As teachers, both Maria and Carolyn were able to encounter the daily struggles children and parents are faced with, in trying to follow and adhere to a healthy and nutritious lifestyle.

As a doctor, Carolina was able to see the consequences of poor and unhealthy nutrition in her patients.

The three authors came together with the purpose of creating a fun character that would be appealing and relatable and a story that could have a learning effect on both children and adults.

Clementine
and her
SUPER FOOD
Friends

AUSTIN MACAULEY PUBLISHERS™

LONDON • CAMBRIDGE • NEW YORK • SHARJAH

Carolyn Botero, Maria Cohen and Carolina Muñoz Fuentes

ISBN -9789948347279- (Paperback)
ISBN -9789948347262- (E-Book)

Application Number: MC-10-01-4365068
Age Classification: 6-9

The age group that matches the content of the books has been classified according to the age classification system issued by the National Media Council.

First Published (2020)
AUSTIN MACAULEY PUBLISHERS FZE
Sharjah Publishing City
P.O Box [519201]
Sharjah, UAE
www.austinmacauley.ae
+971 655 95 202

To our families who have always provided us
with their constant love and support.

It was a rainy Saturday morning,
and I was in the kitchen sitting on my
favorite orange chair by the window,
waiting for the sun to shine.

My kitchen was bright and cheerful,
but in the corner, the refrigerator
seemed dark and very sad.

Inside the fridge were some of my favorite foods:
cupcakes, chocolate chip cookies, orange soda,
flavored ice pops, and a plate of delicious sugar-glazed donuts.

While waiting for the sun to come out,
I ate a sweet donut and began to run in circles,
because that's what delicious
– but not as nutritious – foods do to you!

Then I got a little thirsty,
so I had a fizzy orange soda and
began to jump, because that's what delicious
– but not as nutritious – foods do to you!

Still hungry, I munched on a yummy
chocolate chip cookie and began to dance,
because that's what delicious
– but not as nutritious – foods do to you!

Then I sat down by the window
next to my dog, Sprout,
because my tummy was not feeling well.

At last, the rain stopped, and
I saw a beautiful big rainbow.
"You know, rainbows are special because
there's always a treasure at the end."

So, Mom and I followed the rainbow
to a wonderful place full of colorful fruits and veggies.

As we were walking around, I heard little voices coming from a
weird-looking box. I went over and carefully
looked into it...

Would you believe it? Out popped a bouncy apple
wearing a green cape, a cheerful strawberry
wearing a red cape, and a long, strong,
big-eyed carrot wearing an orange cape.

Oh my, what a sight!
Then, they all began to chant:
"We are your SUPER FOOD friends;
we are the delicious and nutritious,
yummy crunchy bunch."

They seemed so much fun and
they seemed so strong that
they made me want to take them home.

And so, off we went.
On our way back home,
I began to have some thoughts...
I tend to get those a lot...
then I asked mom,
"What does nutritious really mean?"

She smiled at me and said,
"Well, Clementine, nutritious foods
are the ones that make us feel good
and keep us healthy."

Once we got home, Mom squeezed
my new friends into the fridge and it made me
wonder if they would be okay inside there.
So I decided to check on them just to make sure.
To my surprise, our fridge now
seemed shiny and very happy.

I quickly opened it and saw all this
commotion going on inside.
My super friends then asked me,
"Where are your fruits and vegetables?
All we see are your delicious
– but not as nutritious – foods."

"I don't like fruits and veggies,
they are yucky, yucky, yucky," I said.

My super friends looked at each other, nodded, and said,
"We are on a mission, to help you make better choices."

The next morning, I woke up and heard my empty tummy
grumbling and growling.
It must be time for my yummy sugar-glazed morning donut...
yum, yum!

As I opened the fridge, the cheerful strawberry
was sitting on the upper shelf smiling at me.

I smiled back, but just as I was about to grab my delicious
– but not as nutritious – donut,
the strawberry said to me,
"For a morning grumbling and growling tummy,
a berry bunch is good to munch,
and it's a better choice!"

"A berry bunch? And why is that?"
"Because a fruity breakfast is a good way
to start your day. They are rich in vitamins,
minerals, and fiber that will give you the energy
to get off to a healthy start."

I gave it a lot of thought and said,
"You seem so much fun, you seem so strong, you
make me really want to try some!"

That morning,
I painted and sang and danced around.

At noon, when my tummy once again
was grumbling and growling,
I knew it was time to go back to my fridge.

I was excited and happy to see
what my **SUPER FOOD** friends had planned for me.
This time, I saw the long and strong,
big-eyed carrot standing at the door.

"Oh, hi there! My dear Clementine,
is that a grumbling and growling noise I'm hearing?
For a noon-time grumbling tummy,
a vegetable lunch is good to munch,
and it's a better choice!"

"A veggie lunch? And why is that?"
"A vegetable lunch is the
perfect match to a cup of soup,
chicken bites, fish sticks or healthy meat."

I gave it a **POWERFUL** thought and said,
"You seem so much fun, you seem so strong, you make me
really want to try some."

That afternoon, I jumped around,
wearing a red cape and feeling
like a **SUPER** Clementine,
all the while playing and chasing Sprout.

After my busy and fun afternoon,
the sun went down and the moon came out.
It was time for supper...it smelled so good...mmmmm!

"But wait," I told mom,
"I need to grab my fizzy drink."
As I opened the fridge again,
now a bouncy apple was in my sight.

It said to me,
"A healthy drink is a better choice!
100% fruit juice, some cold fresh water,
or a glass of milk."

I gave it one last **DEEP** thought and said,
"You seem so much fun, you seem so strong,
you really make me want to try some."

At the end of the day,
Mom, Dad, Sprout, and I
were sitting at the table
while I told them all about my day.

I said,
"I felt so smart,
I felt so strong,
and my tummy was feeling well.
I felt like a **SUPER** Clementine today!"

And with my cape and yummy healthy food choices,
I'm ready to have lots of fun with my new

SUPER FOOD FRIENDS.

The End

9 789948 347279